*In everyone there sleeps
a sense of life lived according to love.*
—**Philip Larkin**

For David Lloyd
J. D.

*For all at Craigmillar
Books for Babies*
P. B.

Text copyright © 2009 by Joyce Dunbar
Illustrations copyright © 2009 by Patrick Benson

All rights reserved. No part of this book may be reproduced, transmitted, or stored in an
information retrieval system in any form or by any means, graphic, electronic, or mechanical,
including photocopying, taping, and recording, without prior written permission from the publisher.

First U.S. edition 2009

Library of Congress Cataloging-in-Publication Data is available.

Library of Congress Catalog Card Number 2008935653

ISBN 978-0-7636-4274-7

10 9 8 7 6 5 4 3 2 1

Printed in China

This book was typeset in Gill Sans Schoolbook.
The illustrations were done in ink and watercolor.

Candlewick Press
99 Dover Street
Somerville, Massachusetts 02144

visit us at www.candlewick.com

oddly

joyce
dunbar

illustrated by

patrick
benson

CANDLEWICK PRESS

Round and round in circles went the Lostlet.
"Where am I? Where am I? Where am I?" he sighed.
He twirled a big golden leaf in his hand.
"What I hope . . . What I hope . . . What I hope . . ."
But he didn't know what he hoped for,
so he fell silent.

In and out of shadows skipped the Strangelet.

"What am I? What am I? What am I?" he murmured.

He held a smooth white pebble in his hand.

"What I dream . . . What I dream . . . What I dream . . ."

But he didn't know what he dreamed of,

so he was quiet.

Dancing in the wavelets went the Oddlet.
"Who am I? Who am I? Who am I?" he whispered.
He listened to the pink shell at his ear.
"What I wish . . . What I wish . . . What I wish . . ."
But he didn't know what he wished for,
so he stood still.

Running down the road came the little boy.
"Where am I? What am I? Who am I?" he cried.

The Lostlet stopped in his tracks.

The Strangelet blinked with surprise.

The Oddlet
rolled right over.

What was this? Who was this?
How did he come to be here —
stranger, odder, and more lost than they?

A boy. Never in their lost, strange, odd little worlds had they ever seen a boy.

The little boy sat down and cried.
The Lostlet ran up to him.
"Hush!" he murmured.
The Strangelet sat beside him.
"Shush!" he whispered.
The Oddlet peered up at the boy.
"What's that noise you are making?" he asked.

"I'm lost," said the boy.
"I ran away so far
that I can't find my way home."

"Home?" said the Lostlet. "What means *home?*"
"Home is where I live," said the boy.

"Live?" said the Strangelet. "What means *live?*"
"I want my mom," sniffed the boy.

"Mom?" said the Oddlet. "What means *mom?*"
The boy cried louder than ever.

"I want some love," he sobbed.

"Love? What means *love?*" said the Strangelet.

"Can you hold it?" asked the Lostlet.
"Can you twirl it?" asked the Strangelet.
"Can you hear it?" asked the Oddlet.

The boy blinked back his tears.

"Love is what makes you better," said the boy.

"I don't know about love," said the Lostlet, "but you can have my golden leaf to twirl. It's my twirliest leaf."

"And you can have my white pebble to hold," said the Strangelet. "It's my favorite pebble."

"And you can put my pink shell to your ear," said the Oddlet. "It's my best shell."

The little boy stopped crying.
He twirled the golden leaf.
He held the white pebble.
He put the pink shell to his ear.

To the Oddlet he gave a hug.

The Oddlet went very pink.

"So that's what I've been wishing for," he said.

"I'm a Huglet!"

To the Strangelet he gave a snuggle.
The Strangelet felt a deep, warm glow.
"So that's what I've been dreaming of,"
he chuckled. "I'm a Snuglet!"

He took the Lostlet by the hand.
The Lostlet gave a shy smile.
"So that's what I've been hoping for," he said.
"I'm a Foundlet!"

Dancing in a ring, they sang a little song.

"A Huglet am I, odd though I be;
a Snuglet so strange you never did see;
Lostlets no more, all found are we.
How we hope . . .

    how we wish . . .

        how we dream . . ."

"To be H O M E," finished the boy
with a twirl of the
golden leaf.

Strangely . . .
    Suddenly . . .
        Oddly . . .

they **w e r e** home . . .

just in time for supper!